MW01094384

To Kearrah

JUDY COX

Now We Can Have A Wedding!

illustrated by DyAnne DiSalvo-Ryan

Love

HOLIDAY HOUSE / NEW YORK

DyAnne

2006

To my family
J.C.

For pizza in the movies with love
D.D.

Text copyright © 1998 by Judy Cox / Illustrations copyright © 1998 by DyAnne DiSalvo-Ryan / All Rights Reserved
Printed in the United States of America / First Edition
Design by Lynn Braswell

Library of Congress Cataloging-in-Publication Data

Cox, Judy.
Now we can have a wedding! / by Judy Cox; illustrated by DyAnne
DiSalvo-Ryan. — 1st ed.
p.   cm.
Summary: Because the guests invited to Sallie's wedding believe
that a proper celebration requires their specific ethnic food, they
prepare delicacies from around the world.
ISBN 0-8234-1342-X
[1. Weddings—Fiction.   2. Food habits—Fiction.   3. Cookery—
Fiction.]   I. DiSalvo-Ryan, DyAnne, ill.   II. Title.
PZ7.C83835No   1998   [E]–dc21   97-11103   CIP   AC

My sister Sallie is getting married.

She's marrying Roberto Gonzales from 4B. The whole building is invited. Everyone will come. And everyone will bring food to the party. I can't wait! Soon we will have a wedding!

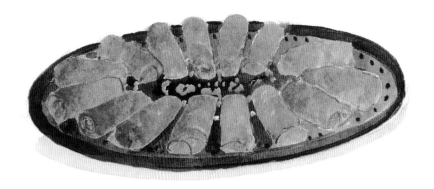

My sister Sallie is getting married.

"What is a wedding without dolmades?" says Papa.

Papa gets out the skillet. I wash my hands and tie on an apron. Papa browns the meat and onions. I roll the filling in the grape leaves. The windows steam over. I give a long sniff. Yum!

"There," says Papa. "The dolmades are done. Now we can have a wedding!"

My sister Sallie is getting married.

"What is a wedding without challah?" says Mr. Gold in 3A.

I wash my hands and tie on an apron. I knead the dough. Mr. Gold shows me how to twist long ropes of dough into braids. When the challah is golden brown, Mr. Gold takes it out of the oven to cool.

"There," says Mr. Gold. "The challah is done. Now we can have a wedding!"

My sister Sallie is getting married.

"What is a wedding without a wedding pie?" says Anya in 2D.

Anya gets out her chopping board. I wash my hands and tie on an apron. Anya hands me a wooden spoon. I mix the kort with meat, chopped eggs, and raisins. The kitchen fills with savory smells.

"There," says Anya. "The pie is done. Now we can have a wedding!"

My sister Sallie is getting married.

"What is a wedding without tamales?" says Mr. Gonzales in 4B.
Mr. Gonzales gets out the steamer. I wash my hands and tie
on an apron.

I mix the cornmeal and water to make dough. Together we spoon on the filling and wrap the tamales in cornhusks.

"White and black beans," says Mr. Gonzales. "So Roberto and Sallie will have many boy babies and many girl babies."

Soon the kitchen fills with spicy smells.

"There," says Mr. Gonzales. "The tamales are done. Now we can have a wedding!"

My sister Sallie is getting married.

"What is a wedding without tai shio-yaki?" says Mrs. Haru in 4C.
Mrs. Haru gets out the cutting board. I wash my hands and
tie on an apron. I wash the fish while Mrs. Haru carefully scales
them.

"The fish of happiness," she tells me. "For luck."

Mrs. Haru lays them out. Their heads are still on. I don't like the way they look, but they will taste very good. We rub the fish with salt and Mrs. Haru grills it over a charcoal fire.

"There," says Mrs. Haru. "The tai is ready. Now we can have a wedding!"

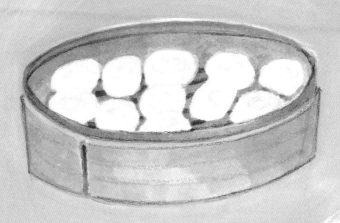

My sister Sallie is getting married.

"What is a wedding without steamed cakes?" says Mr. Chen in 5B.

Mr. Chen gets out his bamboo steamer. I wash my hands and tie on an apron. I beat the eggs.

"Honey-harmonizing-with-oil buns," Mr. Chen tells me. "To bring harmony to this marriage."

Soon the kitchen is filled with sweet smells. My mouth waters.

"There," says Mr. Chen. "The steamed cakes are done. Now we can have a wedding!"

My sister Sallie is getting married.

"What is a wedding without biscotti?" says Signora Theodora in 2C.

Signora Theodora gets out the measuring spoons. I wash my hands and tie on an apron. I roll ropes of dough. Signora Theodora ties them into little knots.

"For two people whose lives now will be entwined," she tells me. She crosses her fingers. "Like this."

I taste some baking chocolate. Bitter! Signora Theodora laughs at my face.

"There," says Signora Theodora. "The biscotti is done. Now we can have a wedding!"

My sister Sallie is getting married.

"What is a wedding without a big cake?" says Mama.

I wash my hands and tie on an apron. I dust the cake pans with flour while Mama creams the butter. Together we sift the flour and mix the batter.

Mama puts the pans in the oven. Soon the kitchen fills with the scent of vanilla. When the cake is cool, Mama frosts the layers and sets them one upon the other, climbing up and up like a white tower. I lick the beaters.

"There," says Mama. "The cake is done. Now we can have a wedding!"

My sister Sallie is getting married.

The counters are crowded with covered dishes:
mountains of dolmades from Papa,
loaves of challah from Mr. Gold,
a wedding pie from Anya,
pans of tamales from Mr. Gonzales,

platters of tai from Mrs. Haru,
trays of steamed cakes from Mr. Chen,
plates of biscotti from Signora Theodora,
and a towering wedding cake from Mama.

All made with love to celebrate the wedding.

But something is missing! What is a wedding without rice? Rice to toss at the bride and groom. Rice to wish them luck and happiness and many children.

I run to my room for circles of net and lengths of ribbon. Back in the kitchen, I ladle a spoonful of rice on each circle and wrap it in the fabric. I tie each circle closed with a piece of ribbon. There, the rice packages are done.

Now we can have a wedding!

Some Wedding Delicacies

Biscotti di Nodo or Italian knot cookies are tied into little knots and baked. They are a tradition at Italian weddings, symbolizing two lives joined together.

Challah is a braided loaf of bread traditionally served at Jewish holidays and weddings. A Jewish wedding reception begins with a blessing said over the challah, after which it is cut and shared with all the guests.

Dolmades are made of lamb, onion, and mint filling rolled into grape leaves. They are a Greek dish served on festive occasions.

Honey-harmonizing-with-oil-buns, an ancient Chinese wedding dish, are a kind of steamed cake. The honey and the oil are said to bring harmony to married couples. Various kinds of steamed cakes are served on many Chinese holidays.

Rice is traditionally tossed at the bride and groom as they leave the wedding ceremony in the United States. Rice symbolizes good luck, happiness, and fertility.

Tai shio-yaki is the Japanese name for salt grilled sea bream. Sea bream (tai), a type of fish, represents happiness. The fish is prepared very carefully, and always served whole, with its head to the left and its belly to the front.

Tamales are a Mexican food. A filling of chicken or beef is spooned into cornmeal dough and the whole thing is wrapped in cornhusks and cooked until hot. Black and white beans are said to represent girl and boy babies.

Tatar wedding pie is from Russia. It is made of layers of meat, rice, chopped eggs, raisins, and kort (a sweet dry cottage cheese) baked in a pie crust.

Wedding cakes were first served in France during the reign of Charles II and are popular in American weddings. Tiers of white layer cake, frosted with white icing and decorated with roses, ribbons, and doves, are an American wedding tradition that has migrated to other countries.